For Sam
K.C.

For Jack
C.R.

HORATIO HAPPENED
Written by Kathryn Cave
Illustrated by Chris Riddell
British Library Cataloguing in Publication Data
A catalogue record of this book is available from the British Library
ISBN 0 340 72268 1 (HB)
ISBN 0 340 71515 4 (PB)
Text copyright © Kathryn Cave 1998
Illustrations copyright © Chris Riddell 1998

First edition published 1998
10 9 8 7 6 5 4 3 2 1

Published by Hodder Children's Books,
a division of Hodder Headline plc,
338 Euston Road, London NW1 3BH
Printed in Hong Kong

Horatio
Happened

Written by Kathryn Cave
Illustrated by Chris Riddell

Hodder
Children's
Books

A division of Hodder Headline plc

Jack threw his slippers
under the bed.

Jack kicked a football boot
under the bed.

Jack pushed his train set,
a drink and a football,
three books, a cheese sandwich,
half an orange, a snorkel
and seventeen comics
under the bed.

Jack went to sleep.
While he slept, something happened
under the bed.

Things sizzled, and fizzled,
and splattered, and scattered,
and while Jack was sleeping
as if nothing mattered
something wonderful happened,

HORATIO HAPPENED

under the bed.

He made his home there –
HORATIO'S home there –
under the bed.

Soon there were mountains
and rivers and cities.
HORATIO made them,
under the bed.

Night after night,
while people were sleeping,
from the home's hidden places
strange creatures came creeping
to watch and to wonder
and soon the word spread:
there's a welcome for everyone
under the bed.

One day Jack's mother looked
under the bed.

She pulled out the football from
under the bed.

She pulled out the train set,
the socks and the comics,
the drink and the sandwich from
under the bed.

Then she saw HORATIO
under the bed.

Nobody knew where HORATIO went to.

They searched down the drain,
in the bin
in the garden.
They found lots of things
that they never expected to –
things with five legs, and webbed
feet, and blue tentacles.
They didn't find anything
quite like HORATIO.

And they missed HORATIO.
They missed him terribly
under the bed.

Every morning, Jack's mother checks
under the bed.
It's clean and it's tidy
under the bed.
No mountains or rivers,
no cities, no miracles,
no sign of the thing
that was once called HORATIO
under the bed.

Look under the wardrobe instead!